MW00773050

ALLIE
AND THE
ICE CREAM
SHOP

BY IANN IVY

ILLUSTRATION BY SASA KHALISA

This Book is Dedicated to
Prince, Olivia & Lucas.

May you grow up in this world giving kindness to all and seek knowledge to build a better future for generations to come.

Black Lives Matter ♥

"Hello, sunshine!"

Allie wakes up each day and greets the morning sun. She lives in Bubbletown with her mom and older sister, Rachel. Before breakfast, Allie combs her hair 50 times to get out any knots.

Rachel is the best sister ever because at breakfast she always gives Allie the bigger piece of toast.

Allie skips out the door to check the mailbox. Across the street is a moving truck and a purple cloud above a cardboard box with legs walking to the house.

What a curious box...

The box lowers inch by inch until Allie sees a mysterious face.

It's Bailey, her new neighbor who looks shy and a little nervous of her new surroundings. She also sees Bailey's cat Pandora playing with some shoestring.

A new face in the neighborhood! Allie wonders, "What could she be like? Does she like the same toys as Allie?

"Does she like to ride bikes?"
Very curious indeed.

At the end of the week, Rachel takes Allie for their Sunday tradition.

They always go to Lickety Split Ice Cream Shop for a Sparkleberry Sundae.

Allie sees Bailey with Pandora, sitting with an
ice cream by herself.

Then two pink-haired girls speak to Bailey...

"Why are you at OUR ice cream shop? Shouldn't you go down to Lavender Swirls for a cone?"

They laugh and make Bailey feel bad.

Allie steps in and confronts the girls in a brave voice.

"Excuse me!"

"Stop picking on my neighbor. She hasn't done anything to you. She's just sitting here with her ice cream. Besides, Lickety Split has the best Sparkleberry sundaes. Everyone should be able to come here and enjoy ice cream!"

The two girls apologize and leave. Allie starts to blush when she realizes that she hasn't spoken out loud to Bailey before.

Bailey thanks Allie for standing up for her. Allie sits at the table across from Bailey. "No problem. They were picking on you because you look different from other people around here. That doesn't excuse their behavior.

To be honest, I haven't been the best neighbor myself. I haven't even introduced myself. My name's Allie. If you need a friend to play with or want to walk to school together, let me know!"

They both smile and finish their ice cream.

The end.

CPSIA information can be obtained
at www.ICGtesting.com
Printed in the USA
LVHW072202201120
672129LV00016B/946

* 9 7 8 0 5 7 8 7 1 0 5 7 0 *